THE
CANADIAN
CIVIL WAR

ALSO BY MATT PAYNE

Millenarianistic Chronodyke
The Sick Book of Lies (with Tom Halford)
Terranomicon
The Adventure Poem of Julius Cinnamon

ISBN: 978-1-7750835-9-7

pattmayne.com

THE CANADIAN CIVIL WAR

SCENES FROM THE CANADIAN FUTURE

MATT PAYNE

I am a purveyor of doom and gloom. A herald of national crises. When times are good I stay in my cave beneath a bridge, like a troll. But when the sweet winds of disunity and decay tickle my sensitive nostrils, I awaken with a smile. It's time to feed on the corpse of hope.

Like all nations, as with all things, Canada is doomed. But each nation has its own special doom. The structure of our strength defines the nature of our demise. Canada is a nation of immigrants, a modern state built by interlopers from Europe and beyond, rabble too uppity to accept their place in their old homes, come to unleash their wretchedness on somebody else's home. Come to build new systems where they wouldn't be losers anymore.

While being too wretched for their original

homes, Canada's first colonial settlers were still strong enough to survive the trip across the ocean. Then they wandered into the woods and started butchering wildlife like savages, and cutting down the forests. Drunken loggers and murderous physicians living among the bears, opening tavern after tavern, hacking each other to bits. Some of them also grew wheat and cows and made lots of money and set up a Human Resources department. Eventually their greed overcame their lust for drunken violence, and Canada became rich and soft.

The most uppity of all the pale rabble, southerners too uppity even for the new society they'd created, revolted violently against themselves. That revolution never actually ended. It's more of an endemic vibe than an event. Now Canada is stuck between those uppity psychopaths to the south (The USA) and normal psychopaths to the north (where it loops around south to the pseudo-Europeans of Russia). Compressed between these pressurized plates,

Canadian culture fermented like fine wine until it peaked with the release of the prog-metal masterpieces "Angel Rat" and "Nothingface," before the HR Department finally took over every aspect of our culture and made everything safe. Now we are a string of isolated cities, so wondrously integrated into the global economy that we are helpless as babes in the woods. And those woods are burning.

The institutions we built to protect us tamed the wild beast of our Primordial Violence and made us too weak to protect them. Now those institutions (which I call the Pillars of Canadian Sovereignty) are crumbling, so our Primordial Violence will be unleashed once more, upon each other. The scenes depicted in this book will vividly dramatize exactly how those institutional Pillars will soon collapse. Without those Pillars we will devour ourselves. Region will turn against region, and we will kill each other for our ideologies. Russia, the USA, and the Climate are waiting to consume the broken pieces of our country. In fact, they are actively accelerating the Canadian collapse. We know this is true because barbarians are already invading our borders, in the form of Joe Rogan and other indie-media cave-persons who eschew the refined mannerisms of polite institutions. That includes me, the narrator, who grew up in the woods, and am currently unemployed.

There are five or six or seven Pillars of Canadian Sovereignty:

- Dairy Superiority
- CBC
- Jordan Peterson
- Healthcare
- French
- Food
- North?

Those Pillars are stacked on top of each other, so it's really one big Pillar, and if one falls they all fall, and they're interdependent, each impossibly stacked upon each of the others, an omnidirectional hierarchy in a non-Euclidean space where this superstacked Pillar loops around on itself and supports itself like a load-bearing many-faced god (where the load it bears is itself).

The following stories are prophesies for how our doom shall unfold. A close study of our own immanent demise can elucidate the possible shape of Canada's future strength.

We will start with Jordan B. Peterson, because he's a celebrity and you have a short attention span. So here is the story of the downfall of Dr. Jordan B. Peterson.

PILLAR N: JORDAN B. PETERSON

Quaim Scrople waited at the intersection in the blistering Ottawa heat until the walk light turned green, then crossed while impatient drivers revved their sweaty engines. Suntan lotion protected the young man's skin. He had a dimpled chin and curly black locks of hair, like a prince.

A stray rock, the size of a toddler's fist, sat in the road between the white-painted lines of the crosswalk. Quaim casually kicked the rock aside and it skittered away from the crosswalk, across the road, over the curb and into the grass.

But how casual *was* the kick? Is any kick really *just* a kick? What deep psychological forces compelled this youth to throw the stone with his foot, like casting a die into the winds of fate? It was the tickle of insult at a symbol of disorder in his beloved city. That rock had no business sitting in the road. It was a driving hazard. A car's tire could catch it on the edge and launch the rock into a baby's skull. *Unacceptable.* So Quaim kicked it away from the zone of danger, appearing so casual and cool, saving the day.

Two pretty young women were crossing in the opposite direction, and they noticed how casually he imposed order on the hellscape of chaos we call reality. They whispered to each other while eyeing him hungrily, curious and slightly afraid. One of them was olive-skinned, dark hair and plump-cheeks with beautiful clear eyes, and she said, "He's so conscientious! I want him!"

He gave them a smile. He was used to it by now.

A car squealed to a stop in the middle of the intersection, burning tire tracks on the steaming pavement. It was a 1994 Chevy Impala, black, and in the driver's seat was superstar professor Doctor Jordan B Peterson. He rolled down his window and shouted, "You! Bucko! Get in the car! We're starting a revolution!"

Quaim pointed at himself incredulously. "Me? Bucko? Revolution?"

The light had turned. Cars were everywhere but couldn't get anywhere because the superstar professor blocked their path. Dr. Peterson shrieked, "Yes you, dammit! I'm recruiting people high in trait conscientiousness, and you're the most conscientious person I've ever seen! Now get in the bloody car!"

Quaim didn't believe in revolutions, but he believed even less in blocking traffic, so he ran around and got in the passenger seat. Peterson squealed off in a cloud of tire-smoke. Once inside the car Quaim told Peterson that he didn't believe in revolutions.

Peterson nodded. "I knew you wouldn't, bucko. That's exactly why we need you. It's really a counter-revolution, so just hear me out! Justin Trudeau has introduced a new bill, called bill X-23, which allows underage manlets to have their chins removed like their hero Andrew Tait!"

"But Trudeau isn't leader anymore," Quaim countered.

"It's a time-bill!" Peterson screeched. "They passed it in Trudeau's final parliamentary session, and it's set to explode into legislation on this very night! Only a counter-revolution can stop it!"

Quaim stroked his own noble chin. He believed in a person's autonomy over their own bodies, but he wasn't convinced that children had developed that autonomy sufficiently to make such a drastic change to their still-developing physiognomy. This time-bill troubled him.

Quaim said, "I share your concern, Doctor Peterson. But I don't completely trust you. I like the old videos of your psychology classes, but since then you've become increasingly unhinged. If you want to earn my trust, just answer one simple question as plainly and honestly as possible."

"Ask me anything, bucko. I'll shoot from the hip."

Quaim asked, "Do you believe in God?"

Peterson's face turned red and the car swerved into oncoming traffic, causing other drivers to veer left and right to avoid a collision. The professor blustered, "God's as real as dragons, man! And if you don't think dragons are real, just ask your nearest five year-old!"

Quaim rolled down his window and asked a nearby five year-old, "Are dragons real?"

The kid laughed and said, "No!"

Peterson scowled, ran a red light, and said, "He's an idiot. A little Greta Thunberg. My kids know better, and they're in their thirties!"

Then the professor crashed his car into a statue of Sir Galahad. The airbags exploded like violent pillows, punching driver and passenger in the face. "We're here!" Peterson cried. He grabbed Quaim by the wrist and pulled him out onto the sidewalk. They were at the Parliament building, where a crowd had gathered on the lawn.

Quaim stumbled and tried to stay on his feet. Touching his sore nose, he saw blood on his fingers. "My head hurts," he mumbled.

Peterson pulled two handfuls of pills from the pockets of his blazer and shoved them in Quaim's palm. "Here, eat some Xanax."

The Xanax was tempting, but Quaim worried about getting addicted to benzos. So he put them in his pants pockets. He wiped away the blood with a tissue he'd been carrying.

The central tower of the Parliament building loomed over the grassy square like an elegant erection greeting a lady's neatly trimmed bush. Peterson smiled radiantly at the phallus and said, "I have plenty of complaints about the state of our country, bucko, but we're still the descendants of ancient virility, an unbroken line of coherent and copulating organisms, and deep in our unconscious lay the symbols we erect to impregnate the chaos of the sky!"

Peterson led Quaim from the sidewalk and onto the square, into the agitated throng of electorate. Men and teenage boys gathered around a makeshift stage. Upon that stage stood a humanoid creature with the body of a man, and his neck reached up to his eyeballs, and in between his eyes were crammed his mouth and nose, all beneath the dome-like canopy of his bald head. Quaim recognized this creature as Andrew Tait. A moat of angry women surrounded the crowd of males shouting their slogan, "Keep the chins! Keep the chins!"

Tait told the crowd, "Being a man is about self-improvement, constant self-overcoming. But these so-called liberal women want to block your right to cut off your own chins! That's not very liberal, now is it?"

"No!" the crowd of males shouted back. Some of them affected deep voices which came out croaking.

Tait continued, "They won't tell you the truth! The reason none of you can score pussy is because of your disgusting chins! The suicide rate among young men has skyrocketed because you've been forced to keep your dirty, pointy chins. But look deeper. Why do they force these chins on young men? Because of the matriarchy! Well the matriarchy ends today! Today I'm starting a new political party. The Incel Party of Canada! It's a haven for male writers whose dreams have been crushed by diversity quotas, and male doctors whose dreams have been crushed by diversity quotas. All the best jobs have been going to women, who won't let you cut off your own chins because then they'd be helpless to resist your chinless charms!"

Peterson dragged Quaim onto the stage and snatched the mic from Tait's massive, ropy, muscular hands. The incels went silent upon seeing their new hero usurped by their old hero. Even the perimeter of protesting women paused their pestering. Many of their eyes focused on Quaim and his prominent, yet graceful chin. It was like they all knew that the future of the country depended on the next few moments.

Peterson pressed his palms together as if in prayer, then touched his index fingers thoughtfully to his lips. Finally he spoke. "Incels of Canada. I came here today to storm the capital, to install this young man as the new leader of the nation, because only he has sufficient trait conscientiousness to lead you out of your own personal hell and into the world of personal responsibility. Mr. Tait claims that you only need chinlessness and pussy, but in fact ladies prefer men with chins! And anyway, you can't just score pussy willy-nilly! Pussy means nothing if you aren't also tackling the maximum amount of responsibility that you can bear! That's why evolution gave you chins and a soul!"

An obese nerd with gray hair and a backpack said, "I'm a sixty-year-old virgin. Society has rejected me! Why should I bother being responsible?"

Peterson shrieked, "To score pussy!"

The moat of women started yammering,

and one particularly shrill lady kicked and punched her way through the soft mass of dorks. She had so many piercings that she was more metal than woman, like Darth Vader. She shouted, "Stop calling us pussy! You think we're just some collective substance to be fucked by the losers whose jobs we stole?"

"Quite the contrary!" Peterson hooted. "These incels have idealized women into an unattainable category, instead of paying attention to the female individuals with whom they could instantiate actual relationships. My message is that only through the crucible of real, individual women, can incels finally enter into the world of pussy, and thereby honor reality by imposing order on the chaos which defines woman as-such!"

The incels and the women erupted in violence. Quaim looked in their eyes and saw neither insult nor opposition, only pure confusion, like chimpanzees attacking a mirror.

The women screamed, "You're a misogynist!" And they grabbed Jordan Peterson, pummeled him, slapped him.

Peterson called back, "No! I love women! I just don't know how to express it except through abstractions! And when I try to apply my abstractions to individual things in the real world I become angry and confused! Aargh!"

The mob tore him to pieces and feasted on his flesh, like a lobster. At that moment, a moment too late, Quaim finally came to appreciate the mad professor. Peterson may have been insane, and corrupted by pride and greed, but he truly cared about the vague abstractions through which he understood humans. He had descended from his ivory tower, benevolently pummeling individuals with abstractions which confused even himself. And now that he was gone the incels would lose all contact with the ancient tradition of masculinity, and fall completely under the spell of grotesque caricatures whose souls were even more empty than their chins.

Quaim escaped the mob by shoveling Xanax into the mouths of anybody who grabbed him. Then he leapt into the Rideau Canal and swam to safety.

Thus fell the nth Pillar of Canadian Sovereignty. But Quaim Scrople knew that it would not be the last.

FUN FACTS!

Alberta premier Danielle Smith claims that if Canada splits up then our various provinces might produce their best work ever, like Wu-Tang Clan[1]. But this argument ignores the fact that Wu-Tang are still together[2]. Instead we should be like Voivod, continuously reinventing ourselves and staying true to the music.

Canada is an abstraction. A conceptual crystallization of pure colonialism, the prog-rock of nations. There is no real Canada, only her[3] provinces, and there are no provinces, only their cities. Each city is its own society, but each of those cities are essentially Canadian. Just as each

---

1   Citation needed
2   Wu-Tang Forever
3   Or his

of my thoughts is structurally haunted by the concept of self, a self I can neither grasp nor let go.

PILLAR N: THE CBC

I still remember the first day of Canadian History class at my high school in rural New Brunswick. The teacher's eyes sparkled with a glimmer of delight as he said, "Okay kids, it's time you finally learned the truth about Canada!"

In unison we responded, "Awesome! We're eager to learn, because only through a public education and the acquisition of knowledge and marketable skills can we ever hope to overcome this rural poverty, which is the hand that fate has dealt us."

The teacher said, "You know how Canada is supposed to be some *socialist utopia?*"

In unison we answered, "No, this is literally the first time we've heard that idea. All of our parents are dirt-poor, half of them are alcoholics or crackheads, and half of those abuse us. Our poor brains are fried. Many of us are already crackheads. Several will not survive the winter."

The teacher's glimmering eyes twinkled with joy as he said, "Well, sorry to *burst your bubble!* But the truth is that we actually stole this land from the aboriginals!"

In unison we said, "Yeah, that's literally the only thing we've ever heard about Canada. We were hoping you might teach us a second thing."

In the decades that followed, many rich people[4] have tried to *burst my bubble* by explaining to me that Canada is not, in fact, a socialist utopia. I still have never heard anybody assert in the first place that Canada is a socialist utopia. But that never diminishes the glimmer in the eye of my would-be bubble-bursters.

But if anybody were to crazily assert that Canada was a socialist utopia (or that Canada was anything at all), they would do well to communicate this idea through the Canadian

---

4   people who own a house

Broadcasting Corporation (or CBC for short).

CBC is the place to go if you want to hear questions about Canadian identity, and what it means to be Canadian. If it weren't for the CBC then probably nobody would produce segments and panel discussions to try to induce the very identity crisis that justifies the existence of the CBC. And what would our identity be then? Nobody would know, just like they don't know now, and that would be a disaster.

The CBC's existence depends on two godlike figures: Rosemary Barton and David Cochrane. Each figure's competence is matched only by their lust for power. Every night Cochrane (a Newfoundlander, if you count the Avalon Peninsula) hosts the Power and Politics show, spending a full hour delivering in-depth political news, analysis, panel discussions, and interviews. While Barton is CBC's chief political correspondent[5], spending several minutes every week bullying lesser figures (like Andrew Coyne,

---

5   Just like Elon Musk is the chief engineer for SpaceX

Althea Raj, and Chantal Hebert) as they struggle to keep up with her blazing wit and profound insights.

Barton and Cochrane circle each other like two neutron stars, and in this stellar analogy the gravitation waves could represent the air waves of CBC radio and TV, or maybe the shows broadcast on those waves. Either way, if those two stars crashed together, or split apart entirely, the very fabric of spacetime[6] would be permanently ruptured.

This is exactly how such an inevitable disaster will definitely soon go down.

INSTITUTIONAL BREAKDOWN

It was election day in Canada. Amid the celebratory brawls, drinking, and stabbings that had taken over downtown Ottawa, one refuge of order and professionalism remained, and that

---

6   Canadian media

was the CBC media tent on the lawn of Parliament. The nation's two greatest political experts held court at opposite ends of that great tent. A flurry of interns and media crew bustled about between them, treading on the soft grass, working under the phallic silhouette that the Parliamentary tower cast on the fabric canopy roof.

David Cochrane, bald as Captain Picard in a fine baby-blue suit, reviewed his extensive notes while performing sound-checks and queuing up with the cinematographers. A phone rang and he answered it, confirming the time for one of his myriad scheduled interviews.

Rosemary Barton prowled the opposite end, looking for analysts and panelists to abuse. But they all knew to keep away until showtime, which only enhanced the anger of CBC's chief political correspondent. She picked up a half-eaten cup of chocolate pudding and prepared to hurl it spitefully at Cochrane, when a more sophisticated outlet for her all-pervasive contempt presented itself.

The tent flaps ruffled, and a lean young woman with short hair and serious eyes entered the lion's den. She touched an intern's arm and told him, "I'm Alicia Thimblewood, the Administrative Ombudsman for the Eastern Division of the Canadian Bureau of Weights and Measures, here for my interview."

The intern pointed at David Cochrane and said, "That's the man you need to-" but then Rosemary Barton shoved the intern aside, sent him stumbling into an array of light panels, casting crazy shadows on the walls of the tent.

"Right over here, Miss Thimblewood," Barton instructed the lady in a voice so obsequiously joyous that none could fail to recognize the threat.

"That's *Administrative Ombudsman* Thimblewood," Administrative Ombudsman Thimblewood corrected. She hadn't climbed the ladder of the viper pit of the Eastern Division of the Canadian Bureau of Weights and Measures by failing to command the respect she was due, or by allowing herself to be intimidated.

Barton's face muscles vibrated audibly in their heroic attempt to maintain a smile and she said, "Of course, my apologies *Administrative Ombudsman Thimblewood*, I've been so eager for our interview! Please follow me to *my* side of the tent and we'll get started right away!"

But Alicia Thimblewood stood her ground. "Actually, I scheduled my interview with David Cochrane, for his Power and Politics show. So I think I'll head over to *his* side of the tent."

And sure enough David Cochrane appeared, splendiferous in his baby-blue suit, charming the guest with a disarming laugh. He said, "Administrative Ombudsman Thimble-wood, you wouldn't believe the organizational acrobatics we had to perform to fit you in, but I told the producers we MUST have the political perspective from the Eastern Division of the Canadian Bureau of Weights and Measures weighing in, so to speak, on the prospects of these fine candidates. Have you eaten? Do you need a snack before we begin?"

"No!" Rosemary Barton roared. "You aren't qualified to interview an Administrative Ombudsman! I am the CBC's Chief Political Correspondent! Me! I'll be interviewing Miss Thimblewood, and that's final!"

Cochrane choked down his fear in a huge gulp, but refused to back down. "B-b-but Rosie, she's m-m-my guest! I b-b-booked her!"

Thimblewood stood with him, her head held high. "That's right, and next time, *Chief Political Correspondent Barton*, remember my god-damned title!"

As they walked back to Cochrane's side of the tent, laughing and chatting together like old friends, Rosemary Barton realized that she still held the pudding cup in her powerful, trembling hand. She roared, "You east coast hick!" and hurled the pudding cup at her colleague. It twirled through the air as Cochrane turned around to face his abuser's taunt. The pudding splashed across his chest, rendering the serene blue suit into a Jackson Pollack.

"Aww, Rosie!" Cochrane cried in dismay. "That's the second suit you ruined with pudding today! I only have one more left, and it has to last all night!"

This little victory satisfied Barton's rage, so her voice twinkled sweetly with triumph as she said, "Cross me again and your little career will be over, mkay?"

Cochrane had neither the time nor inclination for revenge. Interns appeared like a pit crew to disrobe him, cleaned the spatters of chocolate pudding that had splashed up on his neck, and then adorned him once again in an identical baby-blue suit. He sat at his desk for the interview, and Alicia Thimblewood sat adjacent to him. The cameras started to roll. The director said, "We're live!"

Barton turned away and leaned against her own desk, scrolling through the contacts on her phone, wondering who might be available for some more abuse.

Nobody was watching as an impish fatso appeared behind her. He arose from behind a stool where he'd been hiding for hours, waiting for his moment to strike. The impish fatso took a cup of coffee from the coffee station, then had to duck again for a moment to suppress a giggle, peering around devilishly. Finally he rose up, leaned over Rosemary Barton's shoulder, and poured the hot coffee down her blouse. Then, giggling like a schoolgirl, he did a somersault and disappeared beneath the skirt of the tent.

Barton roared in pain from the burning hot drink. She threw her fists around, knocking over lights, scattering interns. Then she beheld the coffee staining her white blouse. She stormed over to where Cochrane was conducting his live interview in front of the big CANADIAN BROADCASTING CORPORATION sign.

"You vindictive little nerd. It's not enough to steal my guest? You also need to ruin my blouse?"

Cochrane stammered, "B-b-but Rosie, I didn't d-d-do anything!"

"You're going to Reitman's right now to buy me a new blouse!"

"But my show! I have to do my show!"

Barton laughed. "Yeah right, like anybody's tuning in to watch this *Newfoundlanderthal!* I'll host your little show. Watch the ratings skyrocket!"

Cochrane's sense of justice overcame his fear and he stood his ground firmly on live TV, planting his hands on the desk. "Well, no, Rosie. I won't let you do a coup on my show just because you spilled your coffee. It's not the CBC way!"

Barton's nostrils flared and her eyes burned red. "*I am the CBC!*" She slammed her powerful fists down on his arm, breaking it in multiple places. He fell wailing to the floor and she threw herself atop him, raining hammer-fists all over his spindly body. He tried to crawl to safety as interns struggled to pull her away. Barton threw them aside. She picked Cochrane up and threw him against the big CANADIAN BROADCASTING CORPORATION sign, shattering it to pieces.

She raised the word CORPORATION over her head, preparing to crush Cochrane like a bug beneath a rock. "With you gone the CBC will finally be mine!"

But Alicia Thimblewood stepped between them. "This is untenable!" cried the Administrative Ombudsman. "You're both at the top of your game, and with our world at a nexus of existential crises, Canada needs you both more than ever. But it's clear you can never coexist in one government-funded monolithic corporation."

David Cochrane dragged his bloody, broken body across the grass and leaned against the coffee station. "I'm not quitting," he said. "She'll have to kill me first!"

Alicia Thimblewood faced the camera and proclaimed, "By the power vested in me as

Administrative Ombudsman of the Eastern Division of the Canadian Bureau of Weights and Measures, I hereby disband the Canadian Broadcasting Corporation. I'm splitting her[7] assets between Rosemary Barton and David Cochrane. All Canadian media shall now and forever be independent and privately owned!"

An impish fatso cartwheeled into the tent for all to see, laughing and giggling for the cameras. "Finally! My greatest rival is dead! Now my independent media company will get the attention it deserves. I throttled the protocols of the media, which include the emotions of media personalities. No institution can survive my media terrorism!" Then he cartwheeled away once more.

David Cochrane managed to stand. He gathered the portion of the broken sign that said, CANADIAN CASTING, claiming it as his portion of the name of the fractured institution. Rosemary Barton laughed and said, "Well that's

____

7   Or his

appropriate. Canadian Casting sounds like a porn site, the perfect kind of media company for an incel like you."

Cochrane laughed back and said, "I'm too classy to say how perfectly, though anachronistically, the remaining words describe your company."

She scowled, choked back another epithet, and was surprised to find tears in her eyes. Through those tears she saw the blood on her hands. It was David Cochrane's blood, but she knew that it was really the blood of the CBC. She had murdered it with her rage. She wept for the dead CBC, but her tears didn't wash away the blood. A rift had opened in her soul. A rift between her old self and a new self, as yet unborn. The Primordial strength of her ego and ambition had exploded the cultural foundations of her success. She was weaker than ever before. She would have to reinvent herself. She was scared.

The crew split themselves between the two

heirs of the divided corporation. Those whose hearts were ruled by fear gravitated towards Rosemary Barton. The rest chose David Cochrane. But all were somber as they cleaned up the aftermath of the mayhem. Their hearts were heavy, and this was a sad day, because they all knew that the nth Pillar of Canadian Sovereignty had just collapsed on live television. The citizens of Canada faced a dark future. Because when independent media wins, everybody loses.

FUN FACT!

If some Techno-Napoleon unites North America, they will come from Quebec.

PILLAR N: HEALTHCARE AND THE DAIRY CARTEL

Several sick people[8] have tried to trick Canadians into thinking that public healthcare is a Pillar of Canadian Sovereignty. But we don't like to talk about that anymore because wait times have skyrocketed so high that we begin to wonder if we ever had healthcare in the first place, or if doctors are some kind of mythical faerie creature from our Irish[9] past.

Several geniuses have proposed introducing medical bankruptcy as a solution to this problem. But the Canadian Dairy Cartel claims that we wouldn't even need doctors if we would just drink more Canadian milk. And research backs this up. Stats Canada shows that those who consume more Canadian dairy products

---

8   Sick as in dying, not sick as in cool
9   Or Scottish or Arabian

experience fewer broken bones, severed thumbs, being dissolved alive in hydrochloric acid, and getting in car accidents after their brakes are cut after they bought oat milk because they're lactose intolerant.[10]

Yes, the Canadian Dairy Cartel is a Pillar of Canadian Sovereignty. But as the old saying goes, a doctor a day keeps the milkman away. If we increase access to public healthcare, that would ravage the bottom line of the cartel, and our nation would crumble.

DAIRY SUPERIORITY

Maggie Boneham spotted Zieg's Grocery from the road. The store was barely larger than a convenience store, presiding over a small parking lot with cracked and faded pavement. Cruel-looking trees surrounded the store, crooked and macabre like demon-trees. She

---

10 Citation needed

parked. A warm wind whispered in her ear as she walked from her car to the entrance.

Zeig's Grocery wasn't well advertised. She'd heard about them through a friend of a friend. She was here because she was vegan. Until recently, consumers could buy all varieties of dairy alternatives at normal, civilized grocery chains, but the Canadian Dairy Cartel had put an end to that.

Maggie was seeking oat milk, or rather, oat *beverage* (the nomenclature legally compelled through laws pushed by the Cartel's lobbyists). But the oat beverage wasn't just sitting on the shelf, and she couldn't just ask for it. She had to approach a security guard and tell him the secret password. He opened a secret door and she entered a chamber of dairy-free delights. Her mouth watered just looking at the labels. She picked up three cartons of oat beverage, and also some cashew-based iced-cream (or rather, *frozen dessert*). She paid in cash.

Maggie headed back to her car. The wind

picked up, further agitating the trees. Several men emerged from the woods wearing all-black, including ski-masks. *It was the cartel.* She ran. They ran. She reached her car first, locked the doors, and squealed toward the highway. She almost made it, but two of the men leapt in front of her car, sacrificing themselves. Maggie knew better than to show mercy to the ruthless Dairy Cartel. She floored the accelerator, felt the bump as the front wheels rolled over one body, but the tires skidded out on the second martyr and she lost control, crashed into the ditch.

They smashed her side window, unlocked her door, and pulled her out. They bound her with zip ties as a white refrigerated truck arrived. Cursing her in French, calling her exotic slurs like "*tabernak*," they threw her in the back of the refrigerated truck. It stank like fresh milk. She was in total darkness as the truck drove away to destinations unknown.

Vegans are no strangers to danger. They're always under attack by deranged meat-eaters.

Even vegetarians frequently lash out, because they're jealous of those bold enough to take their culinary convictions to the absolute extreme. She pulled the Bowie knife from her boot and cut the ties binding her hands and feet. Maggie meant to leap out the back door. She cracked it open and peered outside, saw the pavement rushing past at sickening speed, and realized it would tear her apart like a cheese grater.

So she waited with the knife in her hand. Waited for them to reach their destination and open the door. She would slash and stab, create a bloody opening among her oppressors, and run for her life. Maggie was ready for the battle. Or so she told herself. She had already killed today. But was she ready to die? Was veganism worth dying for? Maybe she should capitulate. Beg forgiveness and drink their disgusting bovine mammary secretion. The very thought made her retch with whole-body convulsions. Maggie's vomit splattered on the floor and the stink of the vomit masked the milk's malodorous reek.

She heard shouting. The truck braked so quickly that she went hurtling forward away from the door. There was no time to waste. Maggie kicked open the doors and leaped to the ground. What she saw *shocked her*.

She had entered a battlefield, at an intersection near a strip mall. A gang of doctors had erected a barricade complete with spike strip to bust tires. She knew they were doctors because they wore smocks, brandished prescription notepads and stethoscopes. She saw two doctors pin down a black-clad Cartel member to the ground. One of them said, "scalpel" and a nurse appeared with the requested item. They cut open the patient's belly as he screamed.

Other doctors hid behind overturned cars, firing pistols at the Cartel members who hid behind the truck. A Cartel operative lobbed a grenade and doctors scattered. Maggie had brought a knife to a gun fight. She had to get to safety.

She ran across the street to a construction zone, diving behind a cement barricade. A doctor was already hiding there and she recognized him as her own general practitioner. "Doctor Caine!" she cried.

He grabbed her by the shoulder and looked into her eyes. "You're late for your appointment," he said.

"I was kidnapped," Maggie explained.

He took her wrist and pulled her through a hole in a fence, across an overgrown lot, firing his pistol at Cartel members hiding in the bushes. Dirt rained down from deafening explosions nearby. They emerged into a back alley and he guided her through a back door, into his office, and sat her down in a chair.

Dr. Caine put his pistol in a drawer, washed his hands and said, "Now, what seems to be troubling you?"

Maggie answered, "I need treatment for my

diabetes and brain tumor."

Dr. Caine smiled warmly and nodded. "Of course. We can start the treatment immediately. Now, I should explain that we've introduced a new payment plan, which allows us to offer even better treatment than before. There is a nominal fee. The price will be *medical bankruptcy*."

Maggie turned this over in her head. "Bankruptcy isn't a number."

Dr. Caine's smile intensified. "That's between you and the bank, and also between me and the bank, but it's not between you and me. Now, shall we start your treatment?"

"But this is Canada!" Maggie shouted. "Medical care is covered by our taxes!"

The doctor explained, "Yes, but tax-payers collectively no longer have enough money for all our favorite treatments, so tax-payers will have to pay individually for certain things instead. Only really important treatments are covered by the government now, as chosen by the Ministry of Human Resources. So Medical

Assistance in Dying (MAiD) is covered by the government, but you'll have to pay out-of-pocket for your little tumor and your little diabetes."

Maggie felt her soul throttled by a roller coaster of emotions. She felt betrayal, but the policy-makers who betrayed her would never hear her complaints. She felt like bargaining, but she knew the doctor had no choice in the matter. Finally she settled on anger, blind rage, and she opened her oat beverage and threw it in the doctor's face. As he stumbled backward in shock, Maggie opened his drawer and pulled out his pistol. She shot him in the belly and he fell back against the wall, slumped to the floor, tried to cover his bleeding wound.

"No!" he wailed. "You've bankrupted me!"

She ran out the front door and stood in the sunlight, surrounded by the warring doctors and cartel members. It was all clear to her now. The Canadian Dairy Cartel had been right all along. If she had been drinking Canadian milk instead of oat beverage then she never would have gotten this tumor and diabetes in the first place. She had been the true traitor, and this illness had been the cost. Her heart sank with dread and remorse, but the sun shone with this new revelation, the revelation of milk. She found the corpse of a Cartel member and she took his ski mask, pulled it over her head, and crossed over into the welcoming arms of the Canadian Dairy Cartel.

FUN FACTS!

Ontario premier Doug Ford once famously declared, "I've never hugged a tree, and I'm not about to start now. Especially not a burning one!"[11]

The history of Canada can best be understood as a genocide against English-speakers, perpetrated by Quebec.

---

11 Citation needed

PILLAR N: FRENCH

There are two Canadas. But which two Canadas are there? Are there French and English? East and West? Rural and Urban? Rich and Poor? Liberal and Conservative? Socialist and Capitalist? Aboriginal and Settler-Colonial?

Canada is egalitarian. We accept all these dichotomies. Each irreconcilable schism is equal in the eyes of the Governor General. And so when I walk among the diverse crowds at the park or in the downtown streets, I know I am accepted. They don't care about the color of my skin. They don't know what language I speak. They can't see my personality disorder.

Yet each of these dichotomies is a delicate balance, a predatory yin and yang with each side constantly devouring the other. No side must ever triumph completely, lest the balance be toppled and our nation rent asunder. French and English are the two poles on the spectrum of language, a spectrum which is also the foundation for the structure of Canada. Francophones and Anglophones are like two cats in a bag who have tentatively agreed to get along for the greater good of the bag. But if somebody shakes that bag, or if one of those cats gets annoyed for some reason, a bloody civil war will ensue.

ANGLOCIDE:

Henry Williams sat inside the pub and watched through the picture window for Beth to arrive. When she approached the entrance he checked his pulse. "Take a deep breath," he whispered to himself. "No need to be nervous around your own girlfriend." But Beth's green dress would accelerate anybody's heart rate. She entered the

Agincourt Pub, turning heads throughout the most posh pub in Prince Albert, Saskatchewan. Henry kissed her cheek before she sat across from him with a flash of her devilish smile.

He ordered shepherd's pie and she got the boiled mutton. They made small talk as they ate, but the sparkle in her eye told Henry that she knew he was planning something. The tension became too much. He sopped up the rest of the gravy with a biscuit, wolfed it down with some meade, and pulled the ring from his pocket.

"Beth," Henry said, opening the little velvet box. "Will you marry me?"

She feigned a swoon and Henry appreciated the effort. But her smile was genuine as she said, "Henry, of course."

The diamond ring became stars in her eyes as she studied it for a few mesmerized moments. A man at the next table eating a *baguette*[12] peered at the ring covetously, but then looked away with exaggerated *nonchalance*[13].

---

12 Bread stick
13 carefreeness

Beth snapped the box shut and put it in her purse. A serious look clouded her face. She leaned in and whispered, "But Henry, what about *Bouchard's Revenge?*"

Henry scowled. "You know I don't speak French. What are you talking about?"

She pulled a newspaper from her purse and gave it to him. "Read this article."

Henry started reading and was repulsed by what he learned. The Quebec government had demanded nation-wide *droit du seigneur, prima nocta,* first night, in exchange for allowing English-speakers to pass through their province or airspace. Whenever any English-speaking woman got married in Canada, retired politician Lucien Bouchard must have conjugal rights to the woman on her wedding night. "It's the only way to protect our linguistic heritage," he was quoted as saying. They called the law *Bouchard's Revenge,*[14] as payback for losing Quebec's 1995 sovereignty referendum. Parliament had agreed

---

14 La revanche de Bouchard!

and passed the law. They had no choice, otherwise Canada would lose access to its precious Atlantic provinces.

"But this makes no sense," Henry said. "Lucien Bouchard is an old man! He doesn't have the energy to have sex with that many women."

"Keep reading," Beth implored him.

Henry read on. Quebec scientists had made a sexual breakthrough. They learned to capture the power of lightning and turn it into pure sexual virility. Lucien Bouchard could have sex all day and all night as long as he had a constant supply of lightning. First they built a nuclear power plant on the Plains of Abraham to generate lightning and test their initial designs. Then they built a nuclear plant in the clouds so he could travel across the country claiming his rights.

Henry took Beth's hand. "I refuse to share you with that separatist beast.[15] We'll get married

---

15 Bouchard renounced separatism after retiring from politics, but can you really trust the renunciations of a separatist?

in secret!"

"Oh Henry," Beth said, her eyes all aflutter. "I love you!"

They kissed. And the man at the next table munched on his baguette and slurped his blood-red wine, a drink so dark it absorbed all sparkly light.

They got married in a cave behind Hunt Falls, in remote northern Saskatchewan. Jars of fireflies illuminated the dark grotto while starlight filtered through the falls' cascading water, casting a dancing starscape onto crooked walls. In this weird light the two lovers read their vows before a druid priestess, who wore robes, flowers in her hair, and strange tattoos on her face. She anointed the union and watched as Henry and Beth made love on a bed of prairie lilies.

The druid left the newlyweds who held each other until sunrise. The cave's watery mouth glowed with increasing intensity until it seemed like the sun must be right outside. The light was blinding. Henry sat up. "Something's wrong."

"It must be Lucien Bouchard with his clouds of lightning!" Beth gasped. She ran to the back of the cave to escape up the tunnel, not bothering to grab her clothes.

"Wait," Henry said, but she was already gone. He had brought no weapons so he armed himself with two jars of fireflies. The water parted and the blazing source of light entered into the cave. Henry prepared to throw a jar.

It was a drone, a quad-copter holding an umbrella which protected its propellors and a battery-powered halogen light. A distraction designed to flush them out!

"Beth!" he cried, and ran to the back, ascended the narrow crooked cavern, and burst into a scraggly riverside field enclosed by evergreens. Beth, nude and beautiful, was suspended mid-air in a bolt of lightning that reached up to into the sky. The clouds above the field were purple and yellow and roiling with flashes of electric light. These sick cloud-bruises expunged a nude old man wrapped in a shell of writhing blue lightning. It was Lucien Bouchard. He floated down like an electric angel with an erection and a scowl. When he reached Beth he said, "Tu m'as trahi. Vous m'avez refusé mes droits! Si je ne peux pas t'avoir, alors personne ne peut!"[16]

Beth's electric aura glowed hot yellow and her body dissolved into pure energy which Lucien Bouchard inhaled in one huge breath, like Kirby. Only her bones and eyeballs were left to fall steaming to the ground. Henry ran over and clutched her bones, but they burst into dust and blew away in the wind. He picked up her beautiful eyeballs and saw that they'd been crystallized into glass. He clutched them in his hands and he wept for her.

Henry looked up at Lucien Bouchard and cried out, "I'll get you for this, Bouchard!"

---

16 "You betrayed me. You denied me my rights! If I cannot have you, then nobody can!"

Bouchard ascended back into the clouds. "Bonne chance, mon ami! Hahahah!"

The stage was set. In Montreal's *Maison Symphonique* the band prepared to play the opening notes to Offenbach's *Orpheus in the Underworld*. Henry Williams and his crew of offended Anglo husbands had bought this entire row of seats at the front of the second balcony. Lucien Bouchard's special glass box suspended from the ceiling just in front of them, slightly above, full of lightning like a plasma ball.

Henry leaned forward to check the line. His crew all wore fine black suits and fake pointy mustaches. He gave them the wink and they each pulled from their pockets their solitary components and passed them down. Henry snapped the pieces together until he held in his hand a plasma trap box, complete with vacuum tube.

The orchestra struck a triumphant rhythm.

Henry stood. He took Beth's glassified eyeballs from his pockets and screamed, "This is for Beth!" And he threw the glass eyeballs at Bouchard's glass box, and the box shattered into a thousand sparkling pieces. Lucien Bouchard fell screaming through the air. Lightning exploded in all directions. After months of lightning-powered sex, Bouchard was more electricity than man. Henry held the trap's vacuum hose and opened the nozzle, which sucked the fractal lightning bolts into its hungry mouth.

The orchestra played a discordant note as the sheet music flew into the air. Bouchard's shimmering figure tried to swim away from the plasma trap's ravenous stream. Francophone citizens from the row behind Henry started grabbing at him. Henry's crew crowded around him, protecting him with their fists. But Quebecois are no slouches, no pushovers. In fact they're the only seriously politically active province in the country. They pummeled one

Anglo man to a bloody pulp and threw several others screaming over the balcony.

But it was too late. Lucien Bouchard's electrified body was sucked through the vacuum tube and into the plasma trap box. Henry snapped the valve shut, discarded the vacuum tube, and fought his way to the exit. The audience had erupted into chaos. He retrieved his backpack from behind a trash bin and stashed the filled plasma box in the bag. His crew discarded their mustaches, rendering themselves unrecognizable, and escaped into the crowd.

Outside, the city became a madhouse of violence as everybody searched for Bouchard's abductors. Sirens blared. Henry and his crew met at the safehouse where they saw on the news that Quebec's *premier*[17] had declared *Anglocide*. They hid the filled plasma box inside an oversized bottle of red wine and went out again to find the entrance to the sewers, where

---

17 first

they could escape to Ottawa. On the street they saw Anglo shopkeepers being flayed alive on racks. Henry forced himself to ignore their screams. On every corner police officers demanded passersby count to three in French. Anybody who failed got shot in the head. Carts of the Anglo dead were hauled by Anglo slaves to be dumped in the St. Lawrence River.

After several days in the interprovincial sewer system, a light at the tunnel's terminus flooded their hearts with hope: Henry and his crew had made it to Ottawa. They climbed up onto the docks flanking the canal.

A smattering of footsteps pranced gaily down the cement stairs from the road. With dread Henry recognized the jolly Francophone cadence of that stride. He signaled for his crew to run in the opposite direction, but they were confronted by men wearing light blue onesies emblazoned with a navy blue *fleur-de-lis*. More appeared from behind. Henry's heroes were surrounded. "*Touché*," Henry muttered bitterly.

The captured crew were paraded down Elgin Street and pelted with tomatoes and *croissants*[18]. People yelled insults in French. The Anglocide had not been contained to Quebec. Gatineau must have invaded Ottawa and easily defeated the soft, cultureless bureaucrats who lived there. Wealthy residents might have escaped on their waterborne pleasure craft, or else turned coat.

As they nailed Henry to a large wooden *fleur-de-lis* on the lawn of Parliament, he over-heard grim reports from New Brunswick: no longer bilingual, to say the least. The uneasy truce between French and English had col-lapsed. And with it, the nth Pillar of Canadian Sovereignty.

---

18 crescents

FUN FACT!

There is a Torture Dome near Britannia Beach in Ottawa, Ontario. The wails and screams of men, women, and children echo off the curved, corrugated aluminum walls. From the beach nearby you hear screams of joy and laughter, and they mingle with the cries of misery and despair, washing them away. The anguish amplifies the joy and carries it on the wings of eagles.

Some nations export their violence beyond their borders, but in Canada we believe in a gentle reminder, compartmentalizing and internalizing it. On this all Canadians are united. Except for the wailing victims inside the dome. But they get what they deserve.

PILLAR N: FOOD

Can patriotism nourish the soul? Could our nation ever taste as delicious as the particular regions where we grew up? From which territorial scope do we receive our cultural calories and economic nutrients?

The east coast is my home. I identify with the Atlantic provinces. I love the ocean, the little mountains, the accents and the poverty. But I abandoned that home because I couldn't find work. I was economically starving. And now I fear I can never go back. The economic strain broke apart my relationships, turned allies into enemies. I lost my oldest friends.

The fisheries had shut down, forcing many people in my community to join the dangerous world of dirt-bike championships just to make ends meet. And I was the greatest dirt-bike champion in town. But one jealous friend (who threw Daryl down a flight of stairs, causing permanent brain damage)[19] accused *me* of accusing *him* of poisoning his own mother. But I never actually accused him of that. His mother was sick and the doctors couldn't diagnose it. None of their treatments had any effect. She grew thinner by the week and her body was covered in sores. She would wail and scream and collapse on the floor. Often she would be found roaming the streets, naked and gibbering, covered in her own filth. But I never said it was his doing.

He told so many people (often in jest) that I had accused *him* of poisoning his own mother that the other dirt-bike champions from nearby towns became uncomfortable, and asked me why I was still riding with him. He had always hated me. He was jealous whenever somebody laughed at my jokes, and he was jealous of my

---

19   and he would randomly scream "the only respect is fear!", and his dad used to beat him in their trailer out in the woods

dirt-bike style.

I liked his mother, and she liked me. She always laughed at my jokes. Her illness broke my heart.

When they found her body in the forest she had been torn apart by wolves. There was evidence that she'd been sexually assaulted. *He* told our mutual friends that *I* must have been poisoning her. He said that's why I accused *him* of poisoning her (but I never accused him of that). Our friends all believed him (even Daryl) and so I lost all my friends and they sabotaged my dirt-bike, causing an awful crash which ended my dirt-bike career and gave me this limp. I grew up with those people. My sense of humor developed with them. Now I can never go home, and there is nobody to laugh at my jokes.

Anyway, Canadians love food. Without it we would scarcely survive. But one man owns all the food in Canada, and such tight-fisted tyranny of tastebuds cannot tolerate the test of time. His rigid empire cannot last. His greed is matched only by the hunger of our jealousy, and when these two volatile forces meet, the result will be civil war.

FOODOPOLY

The automatic doors swished open and Mr. Boudin and his teenage daughter entered into Roblaw's grocery store. The sight of all the colorful fruits and vegetables that he couldn't afford made his mouth water and his heart ache, but Mr. Boudin put those thoughts aside and instead fantasized about the bagel he would soon purchase for his son and daughter to eat. It had taken three days but he had finally scrounged enough money to buy a bagel for his family. He only hoped the prices hadn't increased again while he was out doing un-speakable acts of crime and bodily degradation to pay for this feast.

He found the bagel aisle, and then he found the bargain bagel shelf. Mr. Boudin looked at the price tag, and his heart sank. When he had last checked, the cost of a bargain bagel was seven hundred dollars. But now the price tag said: "One Woman."

Mr. Boudin wiped a tear from his eye and put the bagel in a paper bag. Maybe he could negotiate with the grocer. He brought the bag to the checkout, which was tended by a seven foot tall, gray-haired dork with a winning smile and happy eyes that were incapable of expressing shame, compassion, or curiosity. Mr. Boudin pulled the cash from his pocket and said, "A few days ago bargain bagels were only seven hundred dollars. Can you still honor that price?"

The cashier spoke, his easy smile unwavering. "Hello, I'm Straighton Easton, the owner of Roblaw's. The market dictates prices, sir, and I am just a vessel through which money and food flows. You can't expect me to bend the laws of economics. It's beyond my power! I'm helpless to do anything but accept the enormous costs you must pay for nourishment. Today the price of that bagel is one woman. Pay me, or else I'll call the police."

Mr. Boudin wiped a second tear from his eye and he said, "I already traded my wife for this month's rent at the bachelor apartment I share with my children, and my daughter is still only sixteen years old. I have no women with which to pay!"

Easton responded gently, "That's okay, sir. It's totally legal to marry sixteen year old girls. It's my right as a grocer. In fact it's my responsibility, and I'm helpless to do anything except marry as many sixteen year old girls as possible. It's simple economics. And once your daughter becomes my wife, she'll have a never-ending supply of bagels. Because I personally own them all."

Mr. Boudin knew that he wasn't smart enough to debate an economist. So he called for his daughter, kissed her goodbye, and traded her for the bagel. At least his son would get to have the entire bagel for himself now.

But when he got home, his son Jason was furious. "You traded my little sister for a bagel? How could you?"

Mr. Boudin pleaded for his son to understand. "It's the economy! I had no choice!"

Jason said, "There's always a choice, dad. We're going to open an independent grocery store, where we charge money instead of women! Just like in the good old days!"

They started growing hydroponic wheat in the tank of their toilet. Within a few weeks they had enough wheat to make a bagel of their own, and they sold it for thirteen thousand dollars. They used the money to buy more toilets, where they grew more wheat, and sold more bagels.

One day there was a knock on the door. Mr. Boudin opened it, expecting more customers. But instead he saw three beautiful thugs, lady-thugs with menace in their pretty eyes, pounding their fists. One of the lady-thugs said, "We've got a message from Straighton Easton. This is what happens when you mess with a grocer."

The thugs pushed Mr. Boudin out of the way, then they grabbed Jason and dragged him over to the bed where they proceeded to sexually ravage the nineteen-year-old boy.

"No!" Mr. Boudin cried. He picked up his phone and called the police. To his relief, three lady-cops arrived within moments. They smelled suspiciously like bread. He said, "Police! These three thugs are abusing my boy!"

One of the lady cops said, "Yes, and a handsome boy he is, too."

Mr. Boudin watched in horror as the police joined in the assault of his innocent son. They'd clearly been paid off by Roblaw's. He closed his eyes and wept. But when he opened his eyes again he was shocked to see Jason Boudin surrounded by a languid crew of naked, satisfied women, and his son had a big smile on his face, smoking a Cuban cigar. Jason said, "These are all my girlfriends now. In Canada, first you get the wheat, then you get the bagels, then you get the women!"

In the hours that followed, Straighton Easton sent wave after wave of women to ravage the boy, but he seduced every single one. Finally Straighton himself appeared at the door. The imperturbable serenity of his rich face was now so distorted that Mr. Boudin originally thought it must be Madonna. Straighton said, "You've bankrupted me! Nobody's willing to trade women for bagels since you started charging money again, and you've seduced my best women!"

Jason puffed on his cigar and said, "Looks like the monopolist has been monopolized. Now you have no choice but to set my sister free."

Roblaw's soon shut all their stores. With Straighton Easton out of the picture, the Boudins were free to charge trillions of dollars per bagel. And they had an endless supply of women with which to pay rent at their bachelor apartment.

Mr. Boudin knew he should be happy since his children were now free and well-fed. But they had just replaced one monopoly with another. After seeing the mechanisms of the economy from the inside he knew that the days of affordable food were gone forever. And with them, the nth Pillar of Canadian Sovereignty.

FUN FACT!

When I was a child my father contracted a mysterious brain disease while working as a chemist for the local oil baron. He was taken away to be studied, never to return. Now the government denies that he ever existed.

PILLAR N: NORTH?

Why am I like this? Why do I flee from joy and laughter, seeking solitude and harsh truths instead? When I look at the Canadian sky, why do I always think it's falling?

It's because I come from the North. Ancient mountains are my home, fog and wind are my countrymen. Search my heart and that's what you'll find. The ocean is my merciless horizon. I was formed in the darkness of the forest.

As a child I was adopted by AmalgaMine Industries. They chose to home-school me. The form of my education was that I had to monitor blithistrene levels at a remote outpost deep in the forests of Labrador. I lived alone in a one-room corrugated-steel shack bolted into bare rock with a desolate marsh to the north, all surrounded by evil-looking coniferous thicket stabbing the blue sky with their spiky green bristles. A loon's haunting call was the friendliest voice I heard for several of my teenage years. When I saw those birds landing on the mirror-like serenity of the wetlands, I would cry. I checked the blithistrene levels eighteen times a day, drawing up the sludge with a crank from a pipe-well in the center of my shack.

I wrote letters to my corporate guardians, telling them I was lonely and that I missed having friends. They responded through the speaker system and said, "Make friends with your increasing uselessness, and your dreams of suicide."

The woods were littered with the corpses of their previous adopted children who had killed themselves. Some of them had stashed their diaries in secret locations, which is how I learned that blithistrine isn't a real chemical. This outpost was a form of recreation for my guardians. It had started as an experiment to uncover an Adamic language in unsocialized children but the psychological results proved more entertaining than educational, and subsequent administrations continued the experiment for pure amusement. Their cameras tracked my wanderings in the woods, and their speakers whispered insults and giggles that echoed in the emptiness. They wanted to watch me die like the others. My deterioration and demise would reinforce their feelings of superiority.

But I refused to die. In that isolated environment my psyche conjured mad alternatives to the social milieu my developing brain was denied. My instincts developed schizotypal derangement which taught me about numbers that I must never use, but also other numbers that would nourish my soul and purify my deeds. I learned exotic prayers. A silent voice commanded me to eat bugs, and I obeyed. I discovered books left behind by previous occupants. I found new horizons in those I read, new powers in those I wrote! I refused to die, and this humiliated my guardians. In the speaker system their insults grew more vicious, their giggles became wails and curses. I heard them kick their dogs and throw their cats.

When I returned to society I could not speak, at first. When somebody spoke to me I would respond with a loon's call, or I would write a book. Thus I honored both the wilderness and human culture. And I would roam the mountainside and take my kayak on the ocean. I was free. But was I still human?

Now at job interviews they can see the cold wind reflected in my eyes. They ask me their questions and I answer with the booming voice of the mountain, and they are terrified. I cannot bear to work anywhere that uses the evil numbers. I insist on only using the wholesome numbers, and I eat bugs, and I weep. Then I return to my cave and my books.

But my weaknesses have awakened my greatest powers. I have written books that have expanded the meaning of humanity. This book will make me rich! I have complete faith in myself!

Canada can learn from my example. If we are cut off from the global economy, we will not die! Instead we will become insane. And we will write great books, like this one! In fact, those of us who have been cut off from the main lines of Canadian culture are the only ones who can revitalize this doomed nation. I am your only hope.

Beneath the surface your heart is still ice-cold, like a gangster. Canadian souls are mountain hermits, fur trappers, fishermen, vagrant explorers. You may live a temperature-controlled life where the weather is merely something to pass through between shifts. But your glacier-spirit never melted. Our feet may dance to a southern tune, but our hearts pump icy cold salt water in a remorseless rhythm. We long for the hard winter, and that makes us strong and insane. We straddle North and South.

But now the North is under threat. Forest fires and the Climate have teamed up with Russia and the USA to threaten our Northern sovereignty. And so our souls are under threat. If the North falls, Canada falls.

ARCTIC WARFARE

Felix Crombart awoke to a chill in his bones and scant sunlight peering from across the rolling stony tundra. His mind was foggy. How had he got here? Why was he alone?

He was laying face-down on the frozen stones. Meat stink emanated from the dirty white bearskin blanket swaddling him. He cast it aside and observed that his expensive winter garments had become filthy tatters. As he sat up, the memories flooded in.

It had been an arctic cruise. He signed up with his *a cappella* group from the office so they could finally experience the extremes of Canada.

They had seen some whales, and that was nice. Then they saw an iceberg and they hooted and hollered like chimpanzees while taking photos with their phones. They wrote new *a cappella* songs about the sea, and they got drunk in the lounge singing their new sea chants.

The cruise ship took them into a fjord. Surrounded by those jagged cliffs, Felix had finally made a move on Samantha. They kissed in the cold. He felt her up through her snowsuit, then took her back to his cabin where they made love. He'd never been more happy.

But as the ship exited the inlet a sudden storm whipped up waves that rocked the vessel. An army of icebergs assaulted them. The engines died. An ice field froze around them, crushing the hull. The passengers and crew escaped onto the ice field as their vessel sank. They marched ashore, only to be hunted by a family of polar bears. Half the people died under bloody claw and hungry tooth. Felix had the idea of making slings from their cell phones and charging cables. Thus they were able to kill one bear and drive the others away. But they had no firewood to cook the meat, so the survivors ate raw polar bear and dragged themselves inland, hoping to find a town, somebody who could radio for help. He told nobody about the flask of liquor stashed in his snowpants. It would be their celebratory drink upon rescue.

They wrote new *a cappella* songs to sing at their campfires. The first ones were chants of defiance and adventure but later ones were monophonic and forlorn. Songs of ice and cannibalism.

The meat ran out and the cold defeated them, limb by limb. He buried Samantha's emaciated corpse beneath a rocky cairn and christened it with his tears. All that was left of the polar bear was its skin which he carried aimlessly into the frozen desert. Seeking lichen upon the frozen rocks for scant nutrients. Every time he wrapped himself up in the grim cloak he expected never to wake.

Now he was alone, and somehow still alive. The sunlight on the horizon seemed to taunt him. It gloried in his isolation, his misery. He glared back at the sun and asked, *why have you spared me?* Felix felt like an ice statue, a work of art carved from what was once human. Was this how nature created her[20] greatest works of art? Take something healthy and whole, then hack it into a stark awareness of the brutality of existence? So that existence itself may finally be appreciated as a work of monstrous glory?

But what was this he saw? Beyond his feet where Felix sat, something grew! Was it a flower? No. It was the sapling of an apple tree!

Felix squinted against the sun, feeling its heat. He took off his jacket and walked to the edge of the hill. The vale below was decorated with dandelions. He may find food after all. But what was that smell? Could it be barbecue? With a few minute's trek he crested the next ridge and

---

20 Or his

saw a babushka grilling skewers of polar bear meat on a great griddle, passing them around to men who had doffed their ushankas as they sat to feast. They were reading poetry in Russian accents, but Felix recognized the words. It was William Blake! Felix wept with joy to hear their merry rendition of Blake's Song of Innocence.

He longed for their companionship, but these were Russians encroaching on Canadian territory. And yet, why should the vast north belong to one nation? There are plenty of barren rocks to go around. Would they share their meat with him? Would he share his wasteland with them?

He marched down to the Russian camp and they erupted with good cheer. He joined them and they recited poetry together. He chewed the roasted meat offered him by the visitors. He plied them with drink (vodkow, a delicious milk-based spirit). He invited them back to his shack, and they followed on the wings of friendship.

But Felix had no shack, and he had no

friends. He had lured them onto an iceberg, which he then shoved off back to Russia. They shouted curses which bounced off his hardened heart.

Yes, Felix loved the Russians, he supposed. But he was still an ape, and stupidly territorial, just like them. If they wanted this miserable desert they'd have to kill him for it. He couldn't imagine why he wanted such a desolate expanse and he had no plans to use it. But he did know that Russia can't have it, and either can America[21].

Come to think of it, those might have been Ukrainian accents. But did it matter? Weren't they all children of the Earth? All singers of the Great Song? Well they'd be in Russia soon, so Felix hoped the Russians felt that way.

Felix returned to the valley of dandelions only to find they had burned down in a dandelion forest-fire during the mini heat-wave. Clouds moved over the sun. Bitter cold returned

---

21 Although American *corporations* can totally have it. They can have anything they want.

and froze the ashes. Felix sat among the crispy stalks. His tears froze on his cheeks as he gathered the ashes and mixed them with scrapings of soil. He found a single unburnt dandelion seed, like a follicle on a delicate hair whose opposite end explodes in gossamer handless white arms reaching out to hug the world. He planted the seed in the ashy soil and watched for the sun to reappear and bless this tiny garden with its rays.

The frozen seed began to glow. A throbbing aura surrounded it. The aura was so faint that it could only be seen when the sun was obscured and darkness blanketed the land. He swore he saw little roots growing beneath the dirt, as if with x-ray vision. Was the illumination caused by a radioactive stone? Maybe that radiation would cause the dandelion to grow into a monstrous tree, some freak of nature destined to rule the North. Or maybe this was some mad hypothermic vision, an illusion, or else a revelation of the future. He leaned close and inhaled the aura. It tasted like green tea and fried cod. His eyeballs were crystallizing in the cold, but he knew his radioactive dandelion would keep him warm. This was his new sun.

Felix improvised a new *a cappella* song in a strange new key. A chant for his new sun. It was a song of the eternal future of Canada, and he knew this glowing rock would record the music within its vibrating light. This was the light of reality shining on all living things, opening up for him to inscribe his soul upon everything. He was singing Canada into the substrate of reality. Felix laughed. Was he really that patriotic? No! He just wanted to sing! His nation was the setting and a character in his songs. A stage to perform great musicals which none may interrupt. He would do with it what he pleased. When Canada was gone people would remember its wars and its songs.

The bravery of Felix was bourne from loss and hardness, and on this day he had rescued and salvaged the nth Pillar of Canadian

Sovereignty. He had been an office-dwelling city-slicker, but the North had rekindled his instinct for life, his musical spirit, and his Primordial Violence. The playful, stupid violence that brought his ancestors across the ocean in the first place. Because all violence is for idiots, and can only be met by other idiots, lamented by nerds and cowards. And as Felix Crombart fed the dandelion seed with the warmth of his breath, his heart warmed by the memory of his triumphant treachery, he wondered, *am I alone?* Treachery could expel the Russians[22], but were Canadians treacherous enough to defeat the Climate? Did they have the musical spirit to sing a new future? How long would the nth Pillar of Canadian Sovereignty stand?

---

22 Or Ukrainians

FUN FACT!

Canada is pregnant with a future too powerful, too terrible, too wonderful for the world to contemplate.

ABOUT THE AUTHOR:

Matt Payne writes comedic novels and adventure novels. He lives in Ottawa.